VADER: VOLUME 2

It is a period of insurgence. The Empire's ultimate peacekeeping force, THE DEATH STAR was destroyed due to an unforeseen design flaw. Without this deterrent, the rule of law is in danger. Chaos looms!

Due to his responsibility for the disaster, Darth Vader has fallen in the eyes of Emperor Palpatine. Grand General Tagge is to command the response to the Rebellion.

Unknown to the Emperor, Vader is quietly pursuing his own interests: the mysterious Force-strong pilot who destroyed the Death Star....

KIERON GILLEN
Writer

SALVADOR LARROCA
Artist

EDGAR DELGADO
Colorist

VC's JOE CARAMAGNA
Letterer

ADI GRANOV
Cover Artist

CHARLES BEACHAM
Assistant Editor

JORDAN D. WHITE
Editor

C.B. CEBULSKI & MIKE MARTS
Executive Editors

AXEL ALONSO
Editor In Chief

JOE QUESADA
Chief Creative Officer

DAN BUCKLEY
Publisher

For Lucasfilm:
Senior Editor **JENNIFER HEDDLE**
Creative Director **MICHAEL SIGLAIN**
Lucasfilm Story Group **RAYNE ROBERTS, PABLO HIDALGO, LELAND CHEE**

Disney | LUCASFILM

ABDO
Spotlight

ABDOPUBLISHING.COM

Reinforced library bound edition published in 2017 by Spotlight, a division of ABDO, PO Box 398166, Minneapolis, Minnesota 55439. Spotlight produces high-quality reinforced library bound editions for schools and libraries. Published by agreement with Marvel Characters, Inc.

Printed in the United States of America, North Mankato, Minnesota.
042016
092016

THIS BOOK CONTAINS RECYCLED MATERIALS

marvelkids.com

PUBLISHER'S CATALOGING IN PUBLICATION DATA

Names: Gillen, Kieron, author. | Larroca, Salvador ; Delgado, Edgar, illustrators.
Title: Vader / by Kieron Gillen ; illustrated by Salvador Larroca and Edgar Delgado.
Description: Minneapolis, MN : Spotlight, [2017] | Series: Star Wars : Darth Vader
Summary: Follow Vader straight from the ending of A New Hope into his own solo adventures-showing the Empire's war with the Rebel Alliance from the other side! When the Dark Lord needs help, to whom can he turn?
Identifiers: LCCN 2016932362 | ISBN 9781614795209 (v.1 : lib. bdg.) | ISBN 9781614795216 (v. 2 : lib. bdg.) | ISBN 9781614795223 (v. 3 : lib. bdg.) | ISBN 9781614795230 (v. 4 : lib. bdg.) | ISBN 9781614795247 (v.5 : lib. bdg.) | ISBN 9781614795254 (v. 6 : lib. bdg.)
Subjects: LCSH: Vader, Darth (Fictitious character)--Juvenile fiction. | Star Wars fiction--Comic books, strips, etc.--Juvenile fiction. | Graphic novels--Juvenile fiction.
Classification: DDC 741.5--dc23
LC record available at http://lccn.loc.gov/2016932362

Spotlight

A Division of ABDO
abdopublishing.com

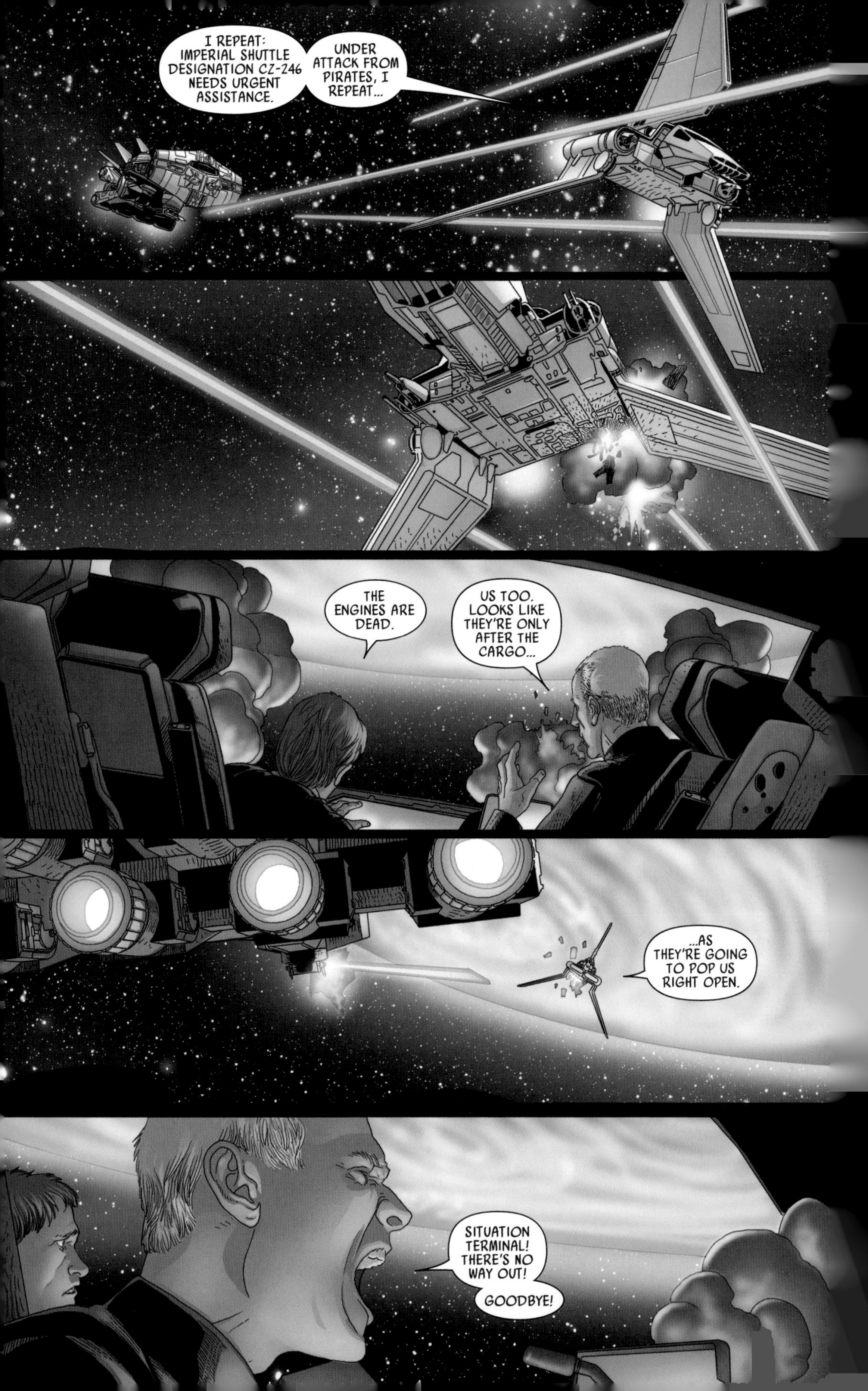
I REPEAT: IMPERIAL SHUTTLE DESIGNATION CZ-246 NEEDS URGENT ASSISTANCE.
UNDER ATTACK FROM PIRATES, I REPEAT...
THE ENGINES ARE DEAD.
US TOO. LOOKS LIKE THEY'RE ONLY AFTER THE CARGO...
...AS THEY'RE GOING TO POP US RIGHT OPEN.
SITUATION TERMINAL! THERE'S NO WAY OUT!
GOODBYE!

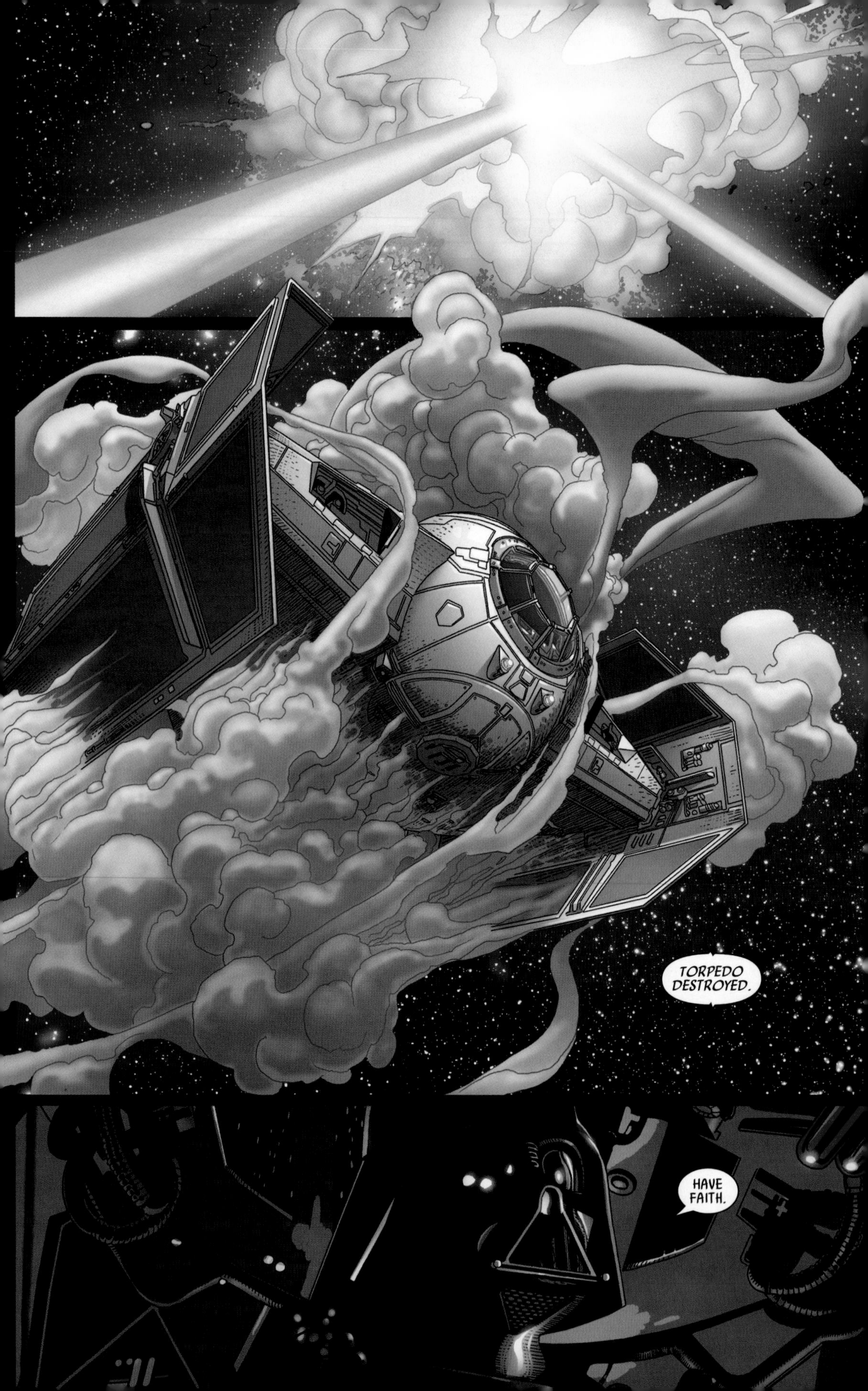
TORPEDO DESTROYED.
HAVE FAITH.

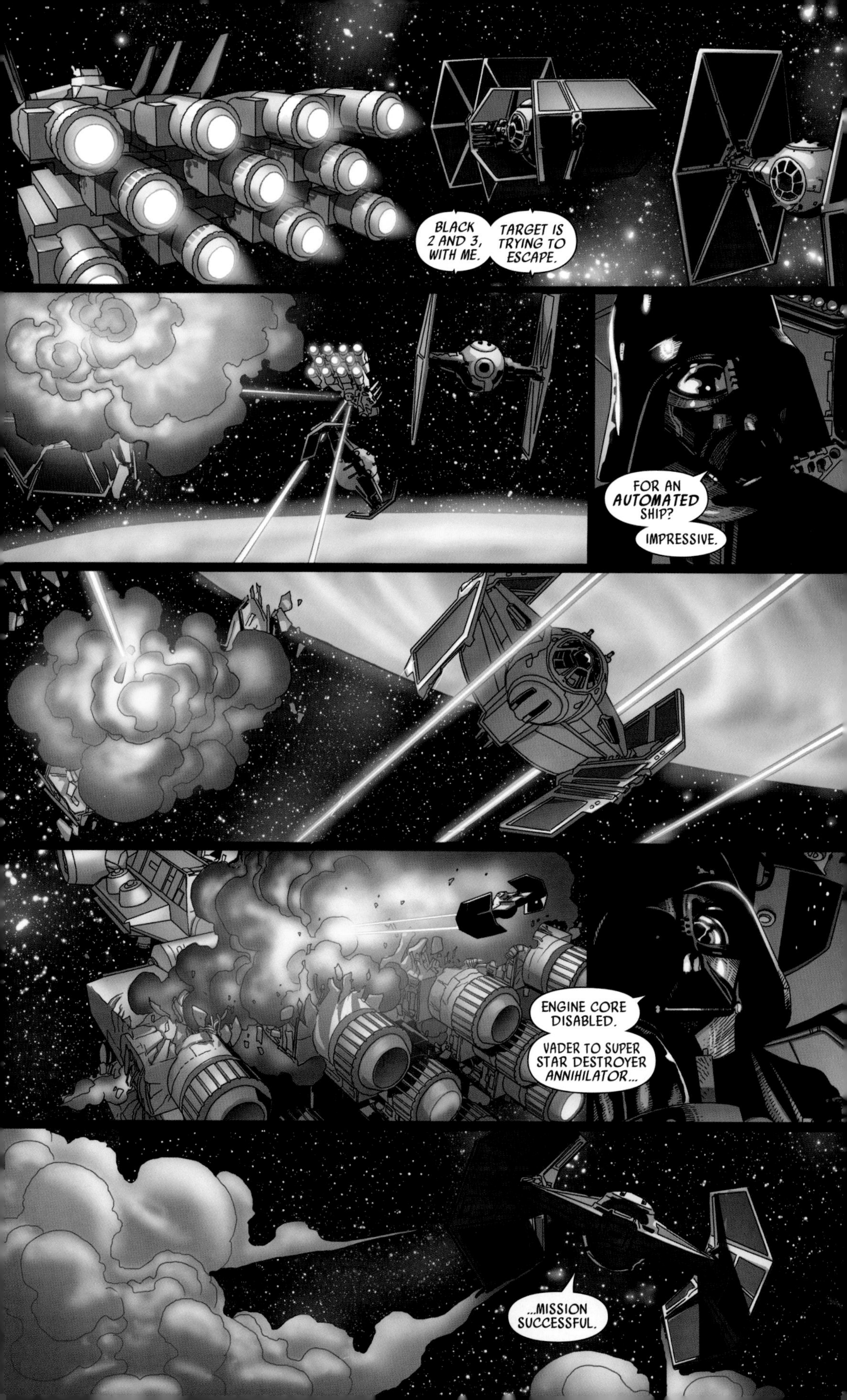
BLACK 2 AND 3, WITH ME.
TARGET IS TRYING TO ESCAPE.
FOR AN AUTOMATED SHIP?
IMPRESSIVE.
ENGINE CORE DISABLED.
VADER TO SUPER STAR DESTROYER ANNIHILATOR...
...MISSION SUCCESSFUL.

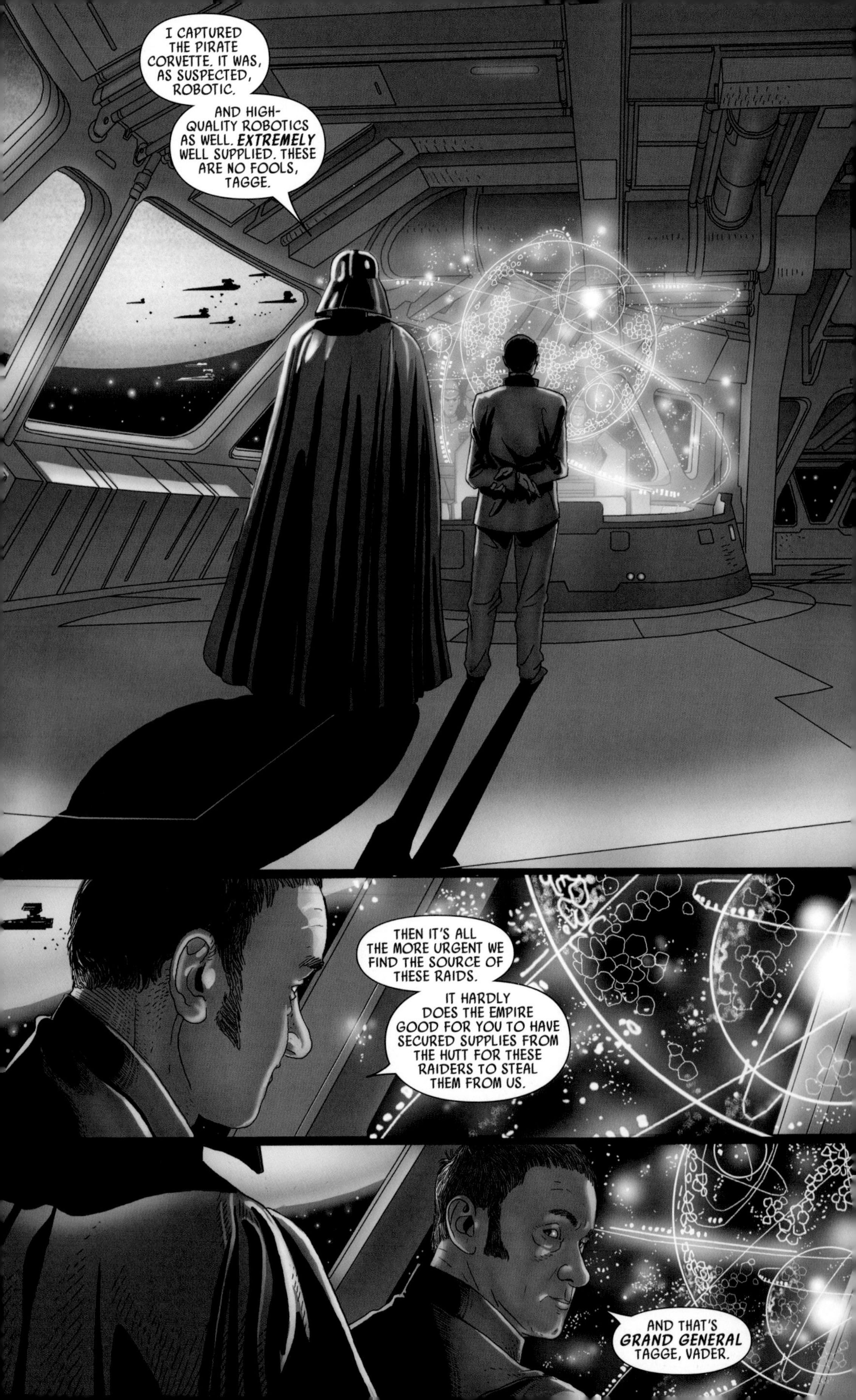
I CAPTURED THE PIRATE CORVETTE. IT WAS, AS SUSPECTED, ROBOTIC.
AND HIGH-QUALITY ROBOTICS AS WELL. EXTREMELY WELL SUPPLIED. THESE ARE NO FOOLS, TAGGE.
THEN IT'S ALL THE MORE URGENT WE FIND THE SOURCE OF THESE RAIDS.
IT HARDLY DOES THE EMPIRE GOOD FOR YOU TO HAVE SECURED SUPPLIES FROM THE HUTT FOR THESE RAIDERS TO STEAL THEM FROM US.
AND THAT'S GRAND GENERAL TAGGE, VADER.

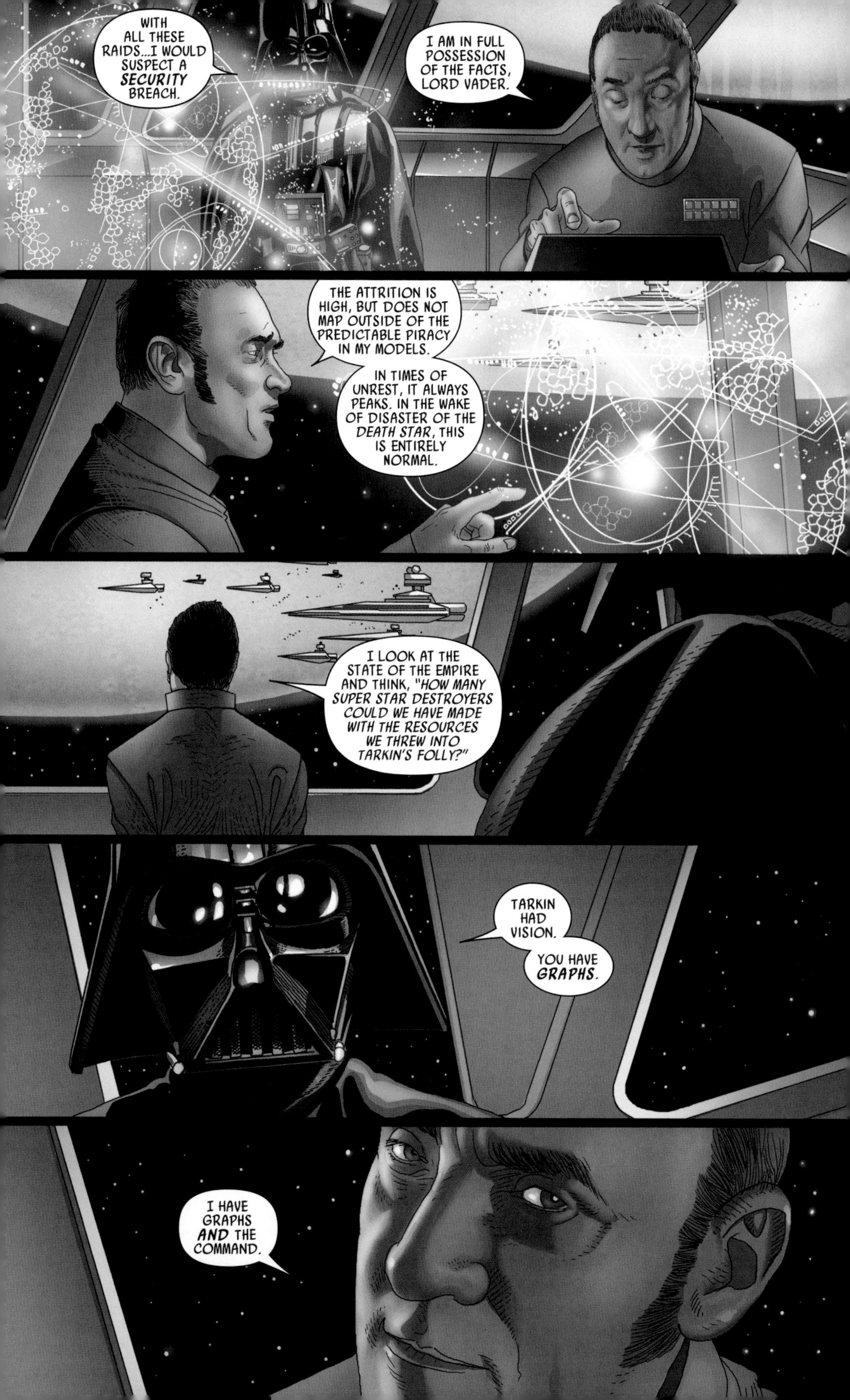
WITH ALL THESE RAIDS...I WOULD SUSPECT A **SECURITY** BREACH.
I AM IN FULL POSSESSION OF THE FACTS, LORD VADER.
THE ATTRITION IS HIGH, BUT DOES NOT MAP OUTSIDE OF THE PREDICTABLE PIRACY IN MY MODELS.
IN TIMES OF UNREST, IT ALWAYS PEAKS. IN THE WAKE OF DISASTER OF THE *DEATH STAR*, THIS IS ENTIRELY NORMAL.
I LOOK AT THE STATE OF THE EMPIRE AND THINK, "*HOW MANY SUPER STAR DESTROYERS COULD WE HAVE MADE WITH THE RESOURCES WE THREW INTO TARKIN'S FOLLY?*"
TARKIN HAD VISION.
YOU HAVE **GRAPHS**.
I HAVE GRAPHS **AND** THE COMMAND.

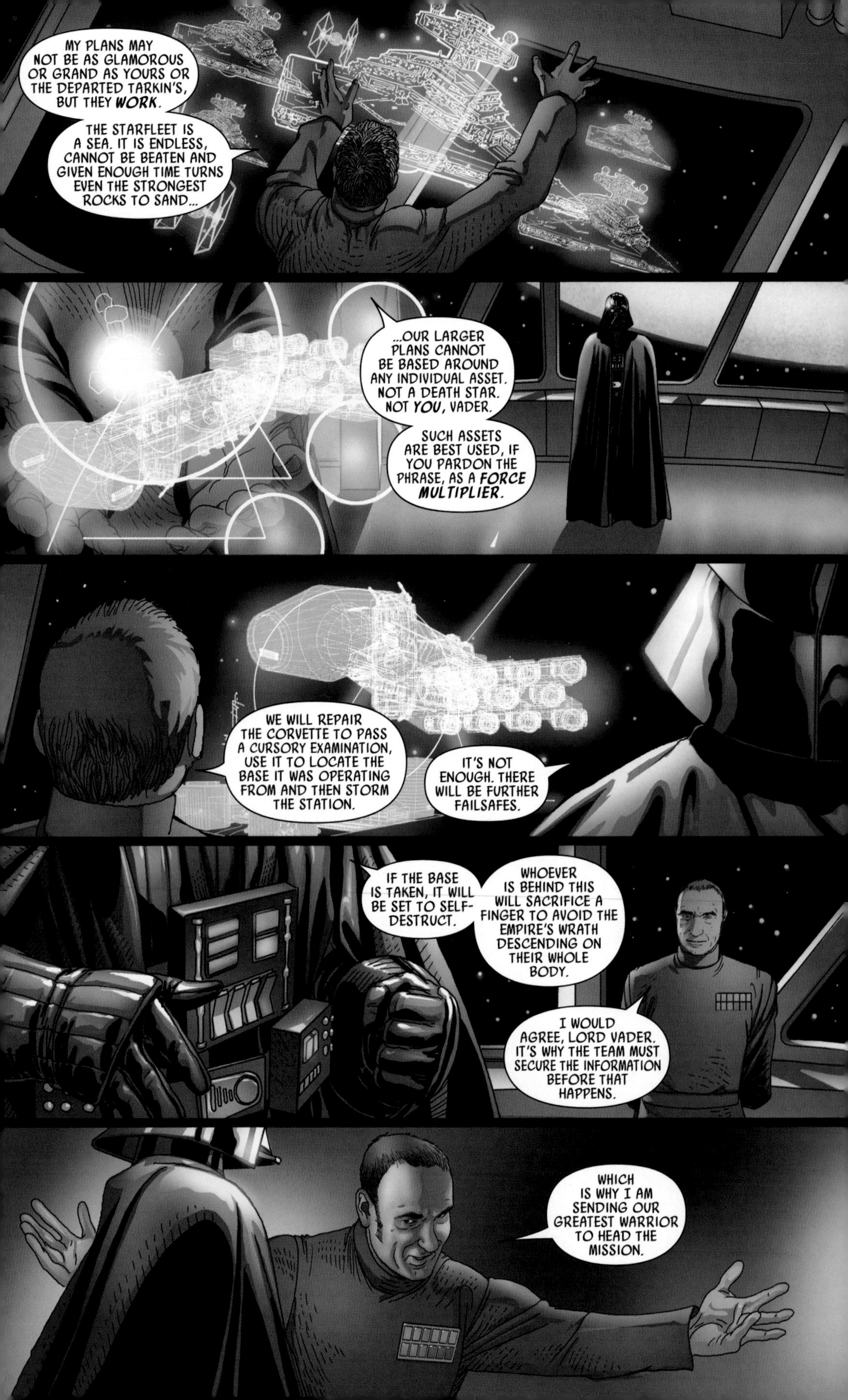
MY PLANS MAY NOT BE AS GLAMOROUS OR GRAND AS YOURS OR THE DEPARTED TARKIN'S, BUT THEY **WORK**.
THE STARFLEET IS A SEA. IT IS ENDLESS, CANNOT BE BEATEN AND GIVEN ENOUGH TIME TURNS EVEN THE STRONGEST ROCKS TO SAND...
...OUR LARGER PLANS CANNOT BE BASED AROUND ANY INDIVIDUAL ASSET. NOT A DEATH STAR. NOT ***YOU***, VADER.
SUCH ASSETS ARE BEST USED, IF YOU PARDON THE PHRASE, AS A ***FORCE MULTIPLIER***.
WE WILL REPAIR THE CORVETTE TO PASS A CURSORY EXAMINATION, USE IT TO LOCATE THE BASE IT WAS OPERATING FROM AND THEN STORM THE STATION.
IT'S NOT ENOUGH. THERE WILL BE FURTHER FAILSAFES.
IF THE BASE IS TAKEN, IT WILL BE SET TO SELF-DESTRUCT.
WHOEVER IS BEHIND THIS WILL SACRIFICE A FINGER TO AVOID THE EMPIRE'S WRATH DESCENDING ON THEIR WHOLE BODY.
I WOULD AGREE, LORD VADER. IT'S WHY THE TEAM MUST SECURE THE INFORMATION BEFORE THAT HAPPENS.
WHICH IS WHY I AM SENDING OUR GREATEST WARRIOR TO HEAD THE MISSION.

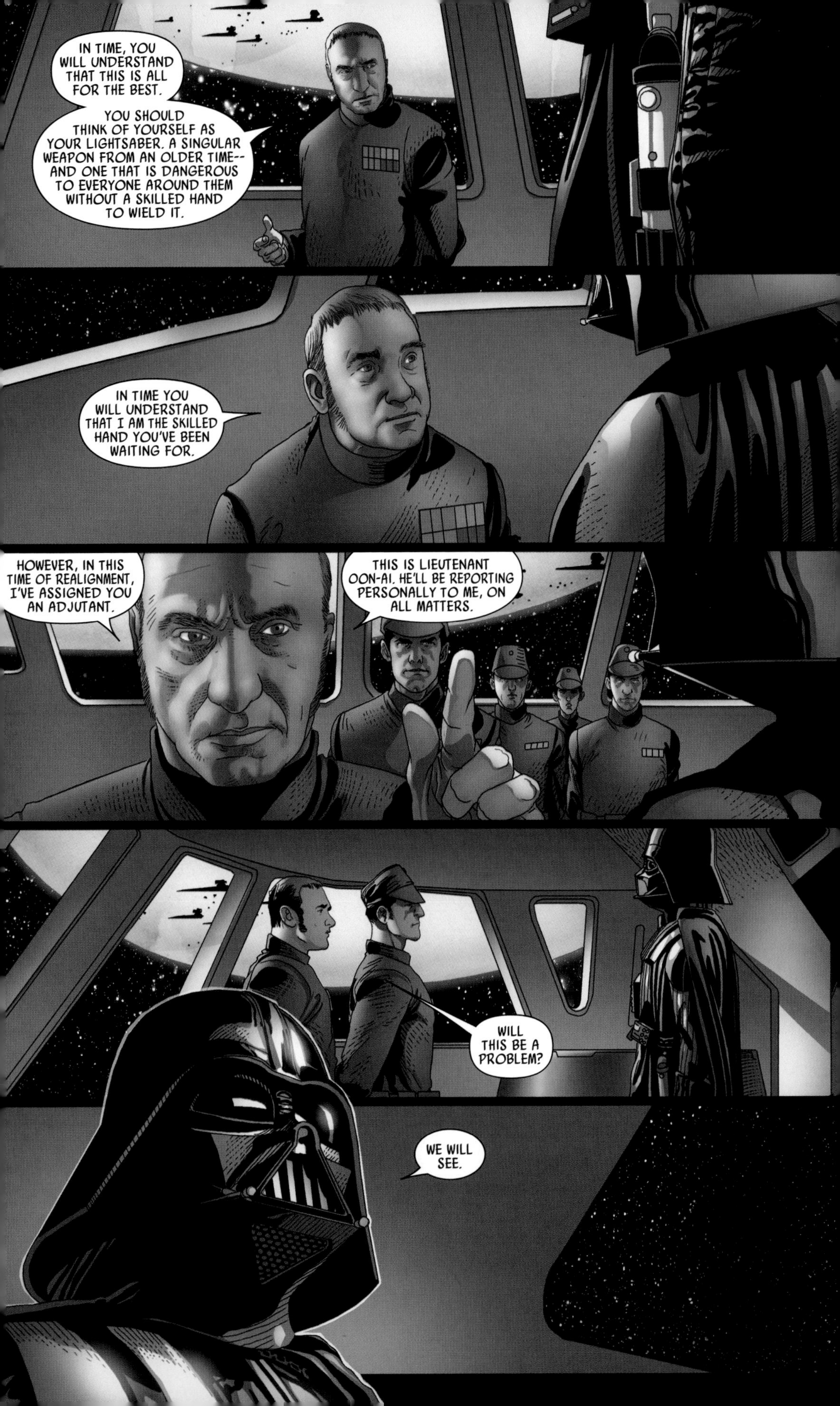

IN TIME, YOU WILL UNDERSTAND THAT THIS IS ALL FOR THE BEST.
YOU SHOULD THINK OF YOURSELF AS YOUR LIGHTSABER. A SINGULAR WEAPON FROM AN OLDER TIME-- AND ONE THAT IS DANGEROUS TO EVERYONE AROUND THEM WITHOUT A SKILLED HAND TO WIELD IT.
IN TIME YOU WILL UNDERSTAND THAT I AM THE SKILLED HAND YOU'VE BEEN WAITING FOR.
HOWEVER, IN THIS TIME OF REALIGNMENT, I'VE ASSIGNED YOU AN ADJUTANT.
THIS IS LIEUTENANT OON-AI. HE'LL BE REPORTING PERSONALLY TO ME, ON ALL MATTERS.
WILL THIS BE A PROBLEM?
WE WILL SEE.

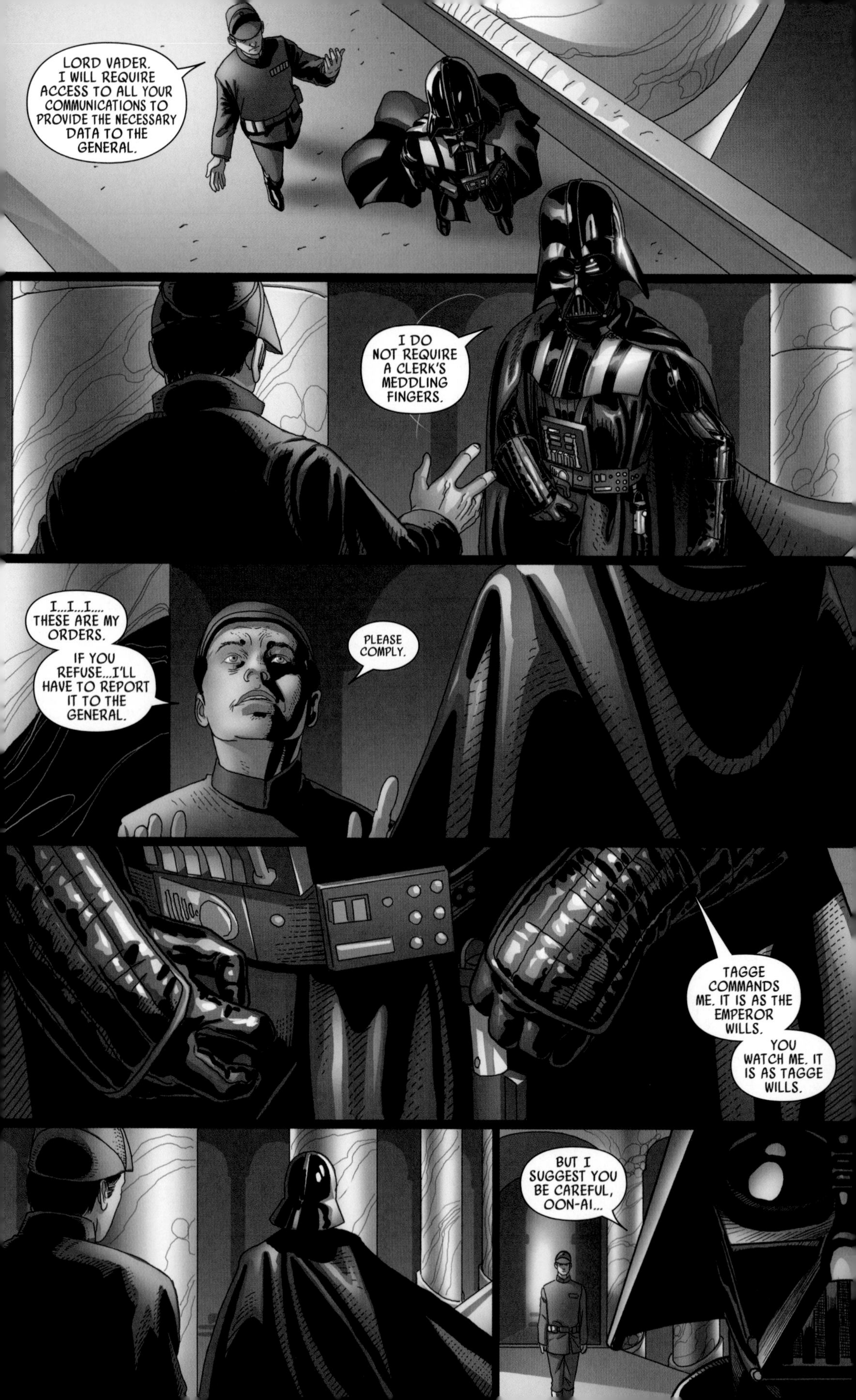
LORD VADER. I WILL REQUIRE ACCESS TO ALL YOUR COMMUNICATIONS TO PROVIDE THE NECESSARY DATA TO THE GENERAL.
I DO NOT REQUIRE A CLERK'S MEDDLING FINGERS.
I...I...I.... THESE ARE MY ORDERS.
IF YOU REFUSE...I'LL HAVE TO REPORT IT TO THE GENERAL.
PLEASE COMPLY.
TAGGE COMMANDS ME. IT IS AS THE EMPEROR WILLS.
YOU WATCH ME. IT IS AS TAGGE WILLS.
BUT I SUGGEST YOU BE CAREFUL, OON-AI...

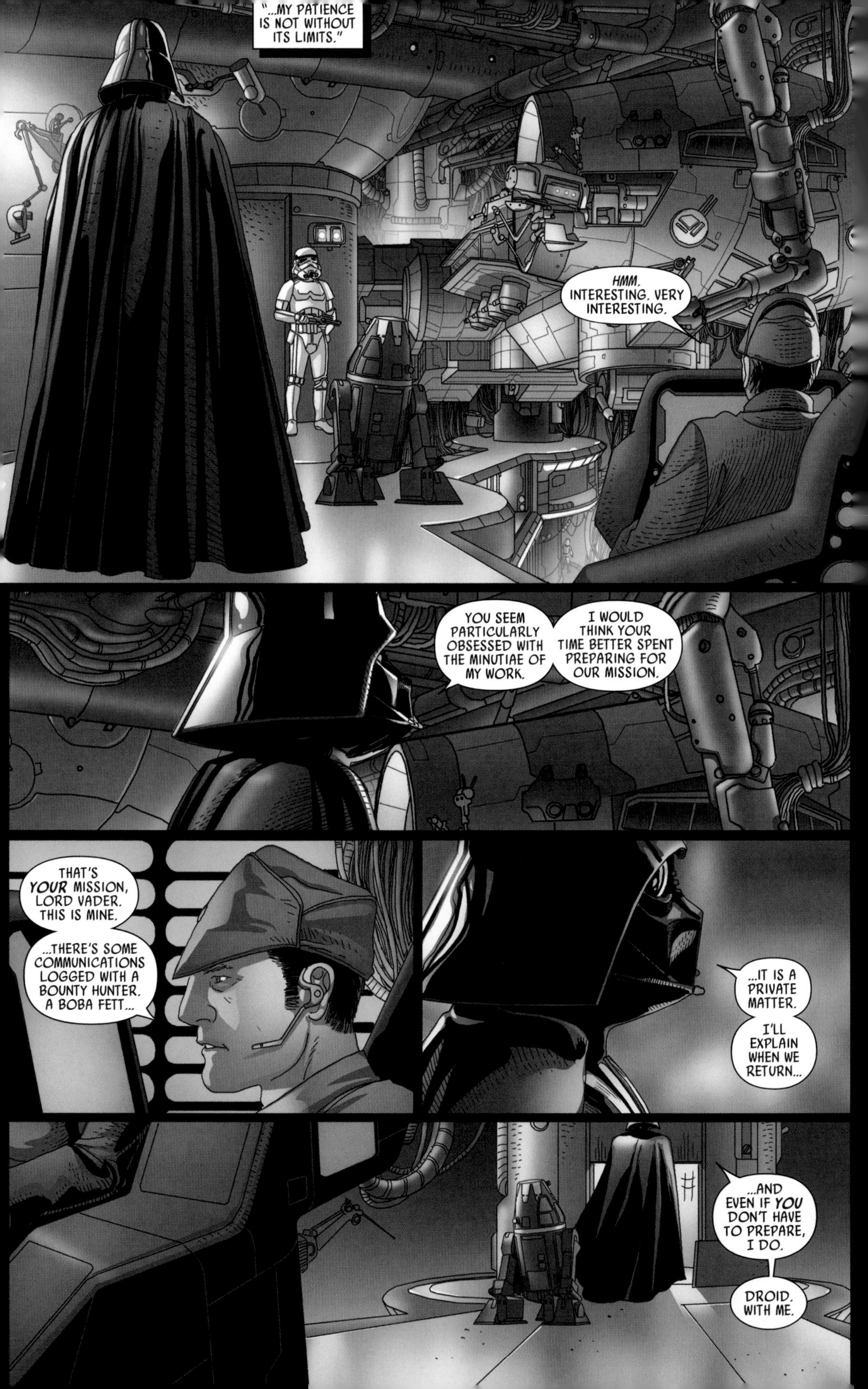
"...MY PATIENCE IS NOT WITHOUT ITS LIMITS."
HMM. INTERESTING. VERY INTERESTING.
YOU SEEM PARTICULARLY OBSESSED WITH THE MINUTIAE OF MY WORK.
I WOULD THINK YOUR TIME BETTER SPENT PREPARING FOR OUR MISSION.
THAT'S YOUR MISSION, LORD VADER. THIS IS MINE.
...THERE'S SOME COMMUNICATIONS LOGGED WITH A BOUNTY HUNTER. A BOBA FETT...
...IT IS A PRIVATE MATTER.
I'LL EXPLAIN WHEN WE RETURN...
...AND EVEN IF YOU DON'T HAVE TO PREPARE, I DO.
DROID. WITH ME.

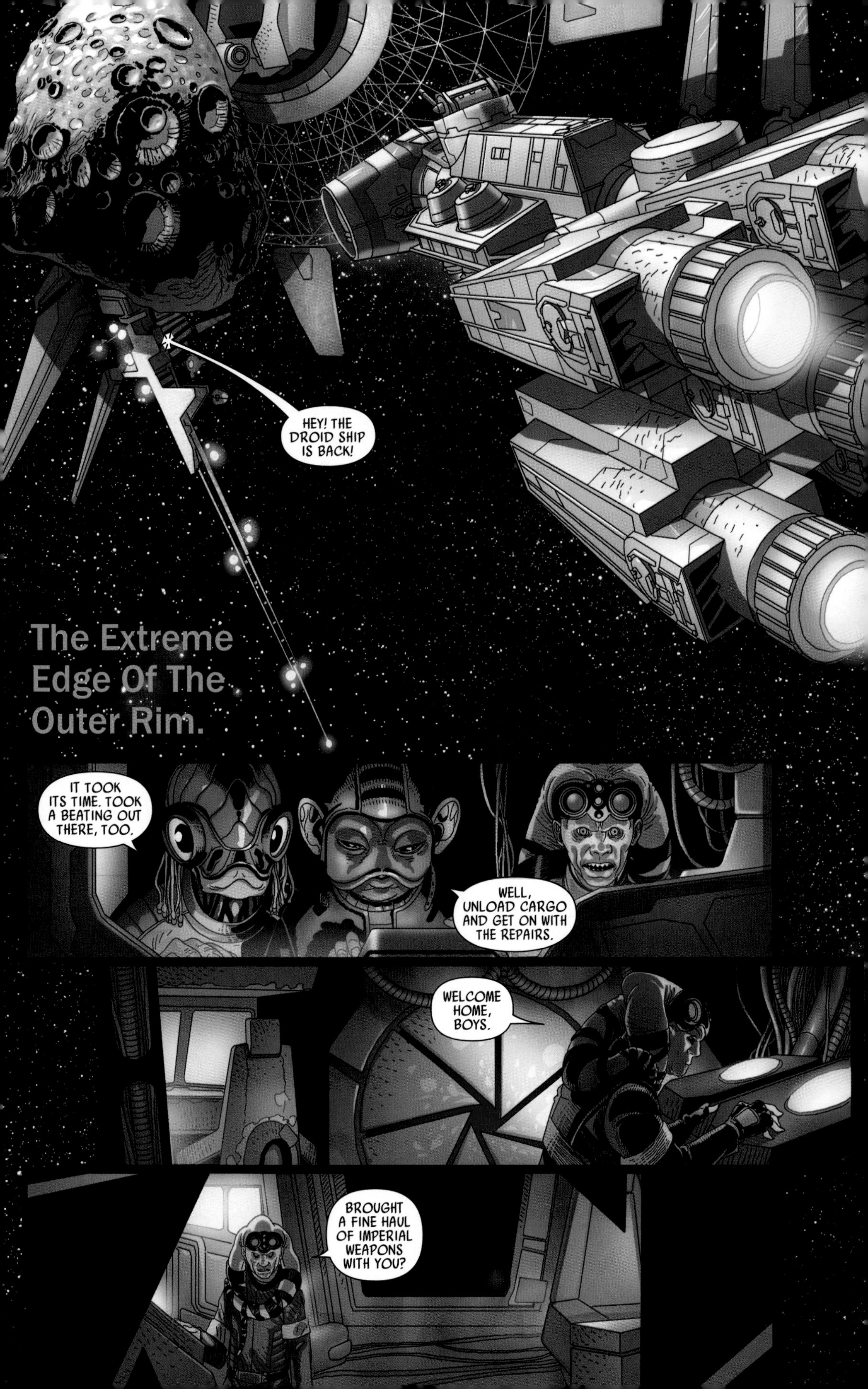
HEY! THE DROID SHIP IS BACK!
The Extreme Edge Of The Outer Rim.
IT TOOK ITS TIME. TOOK A BEATING OUT THERE, TOO.
WELL, UNLOAD CARGO AND GET ON WITH THE REPAIRS.
WELCOME HOME, BOYS.
BROUGHT A FINE HAUL OF IMPERIAL WEAPONS WITH YOU?

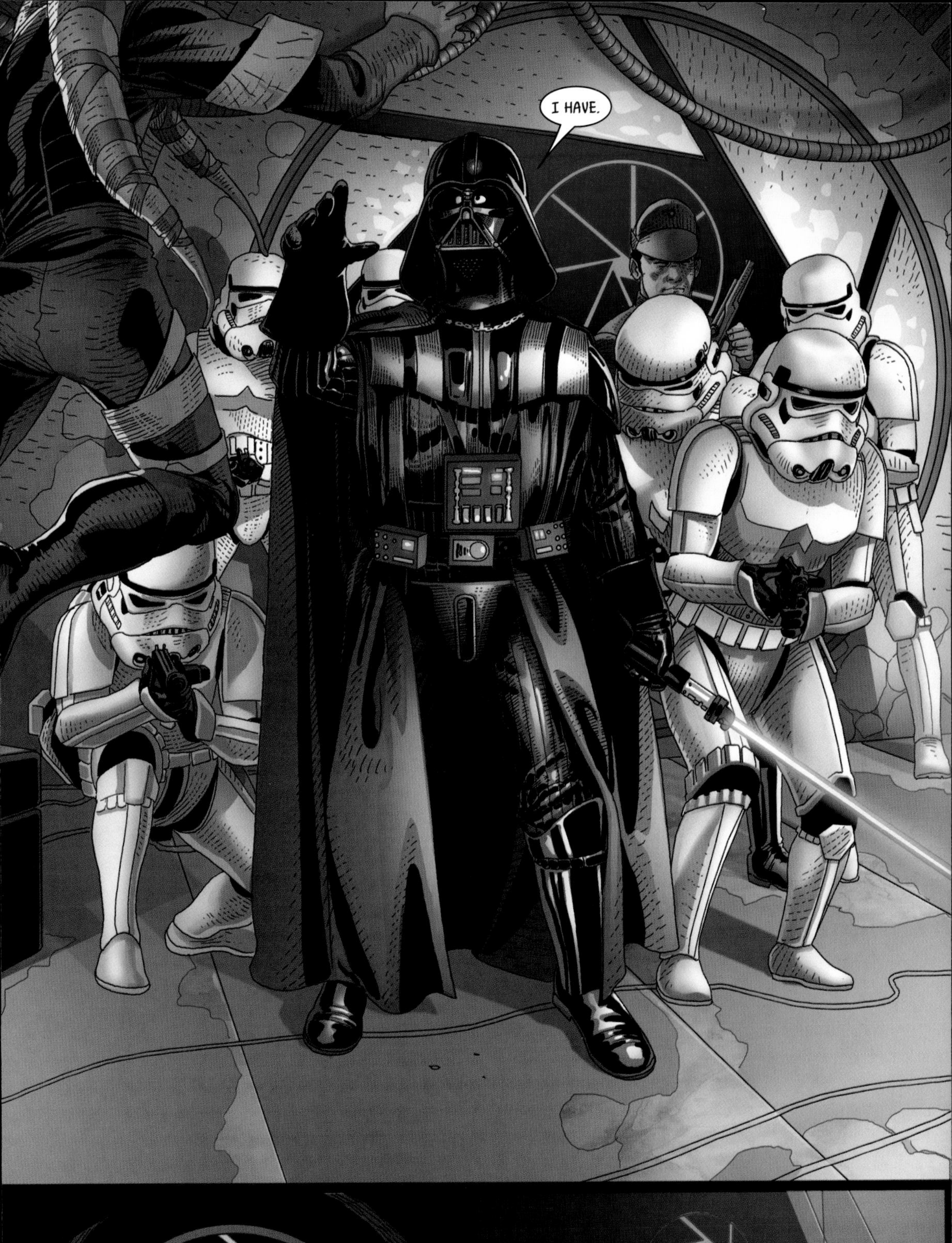
I HAVE.

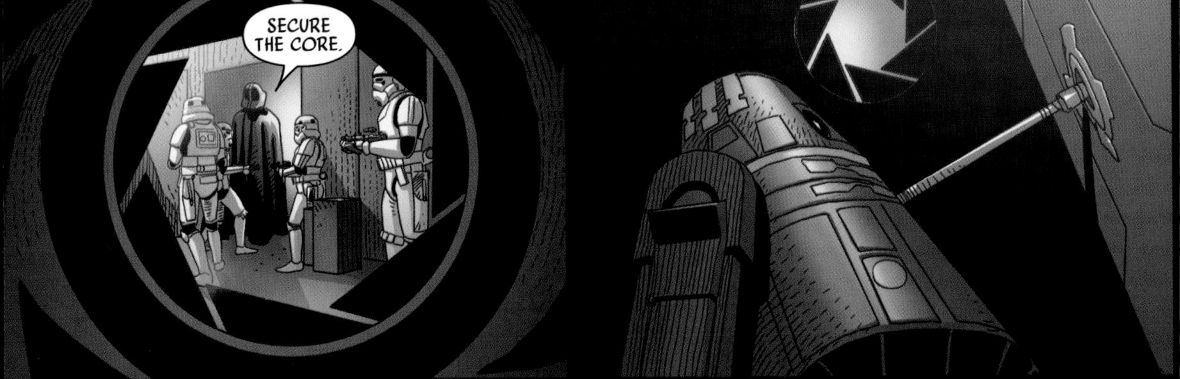
SECURE THE CORE.

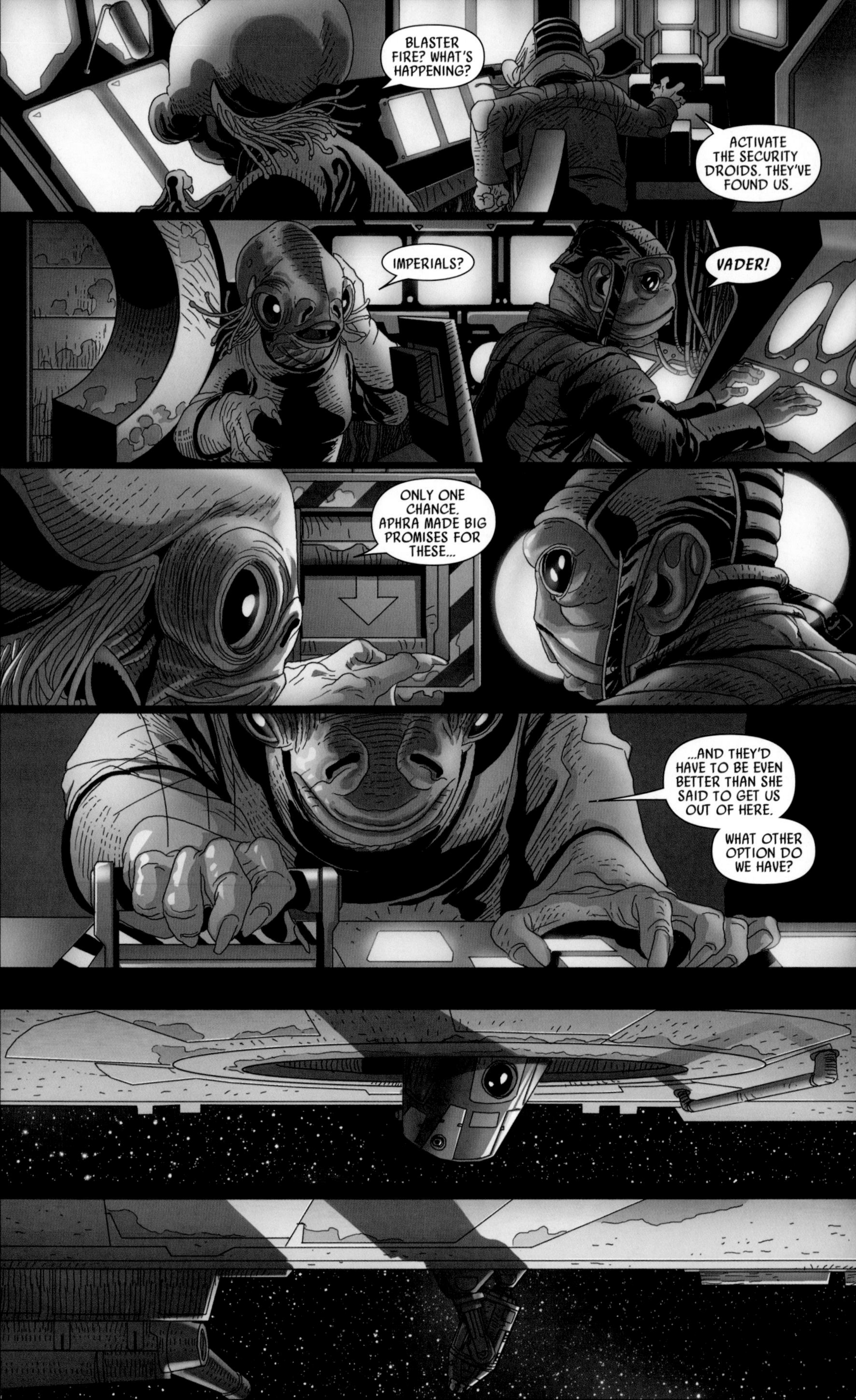
BLASTER FIRE? WHAT'S HAPPENING?
ACTIVATE THE SECURITY DROIDS. THEY'VE FOUND US.
IMPERIALS?
VADER!
ONLY ONE CHANCE. APHRA MADE BIG PROMISES FOR THESE...
...AND THEY'D HAVE TO BE EVEN BETTER THAN SHE SAID TO GET US OUT OF HERE.
WHAT OTHER OPTION DO WE HAVE?

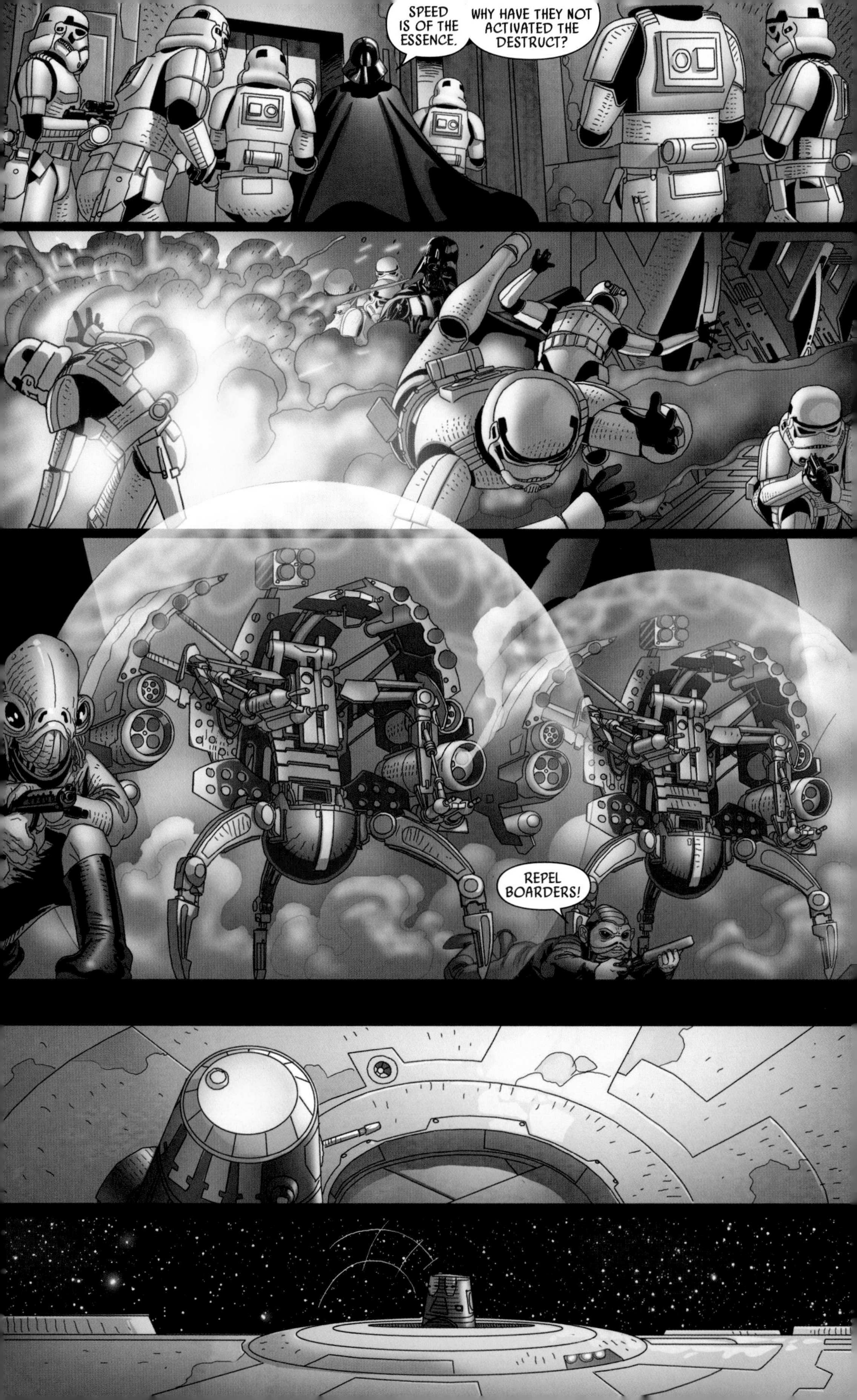
SPEED IS OF THE ESSENCE.
WHY HAVE THEY NOT ACTIVATED THE DESTRUCT?
REPEL BOARDERS!

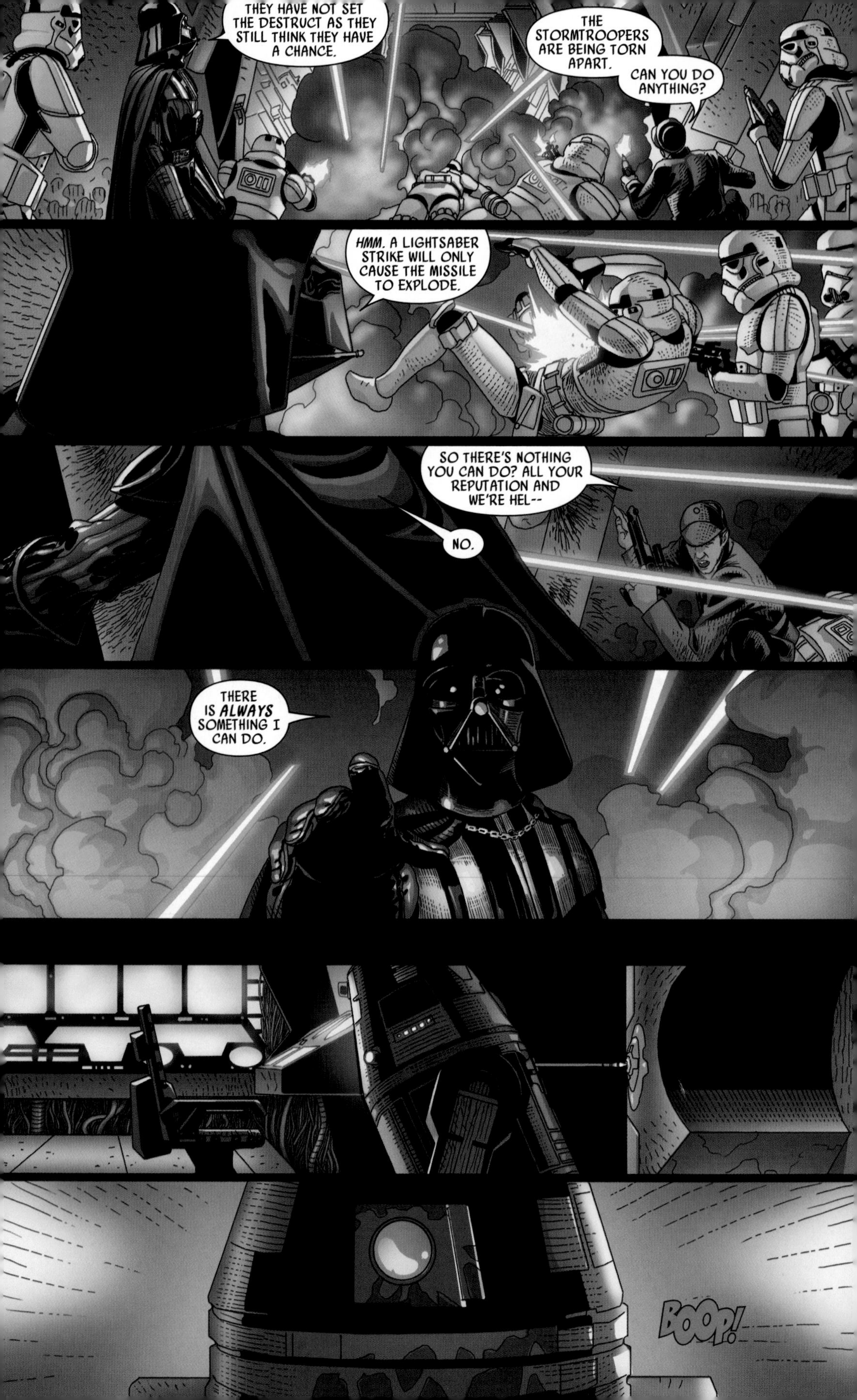
THEY HAVE NOT SET THE DESTRUCT AS THEY STILL THINK THEY HAVE A CHANCE.
THE STORMTROOPERS ARE BEING TORN APART.
CAN YOU DO ANYTHING?
HMM. A LIGHTSABER STRIKE WILL ONLY CAUSE THE MISSILE TO EXPLODE.
SO THERE'S NOTHING YOU CAN DO? ALL YOUR REPUTATION AND WE'RE HEL--
NO.
THERE IS *ALWAYS* SOMETHING I CAN DO.
BOOP!

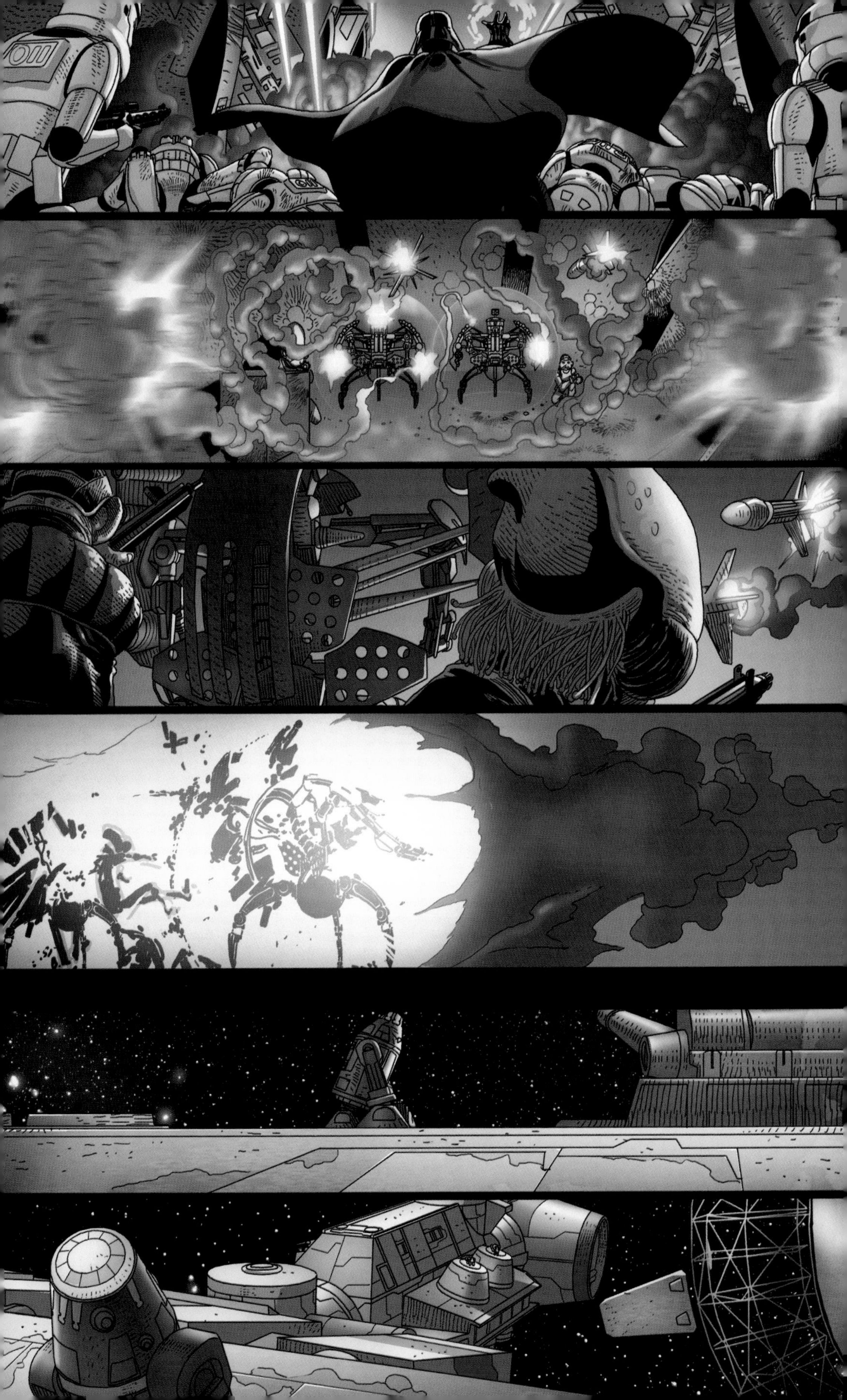

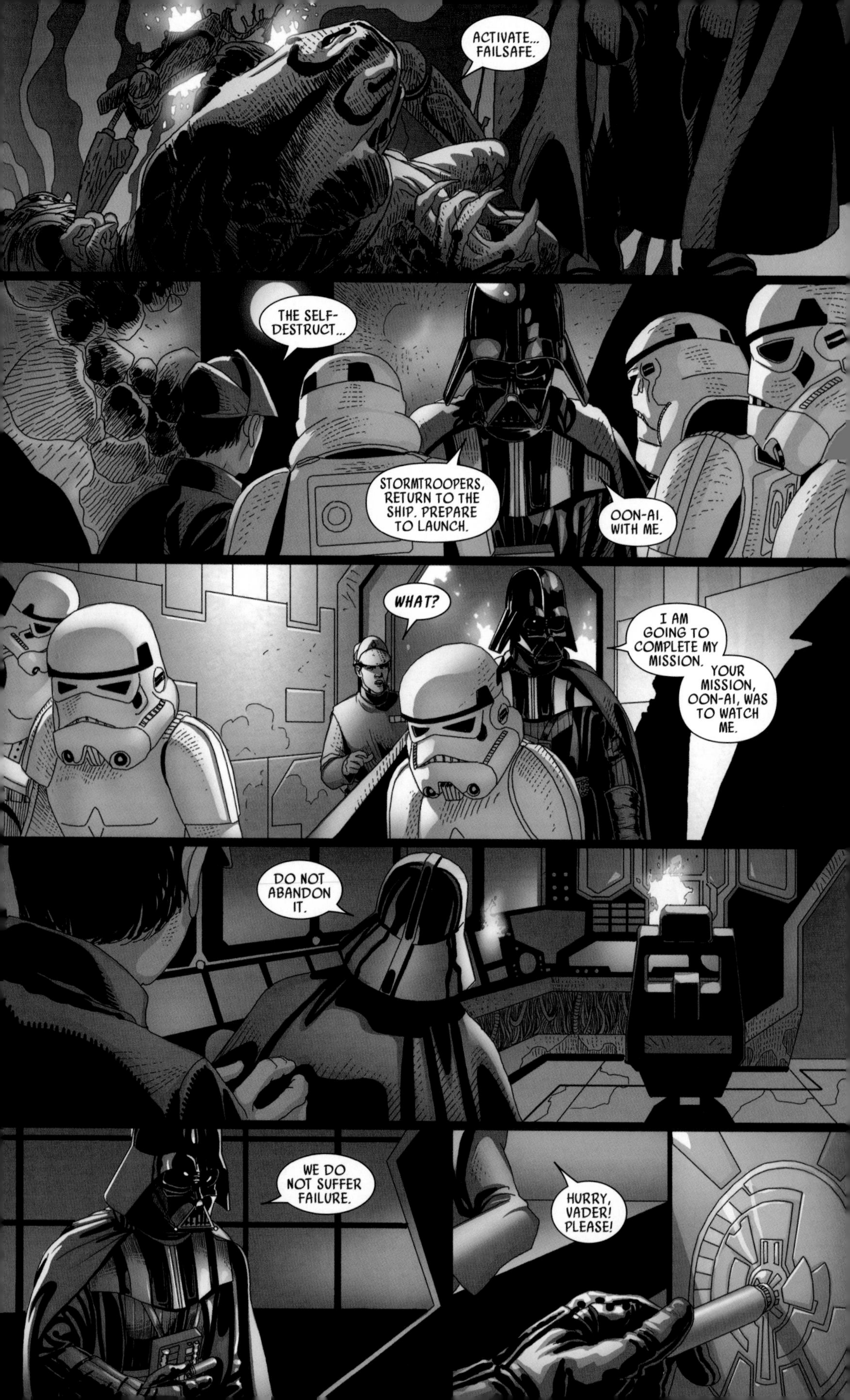
ACTIVATE... FAILSAFE.
THE SELF-DESTRUCT...
STORMTROOPERS, RETURN TO THE SHIP. PREPARE TO LAUNCH.
OON-AI. WITH ME.
WHAT?
I AM GOING TO COMPLETE MY MISSION.
YOUR MISSION, OON-AI, WAS TO WATCH ME.
DO NOT ABANDON IT.
WE DO NOT SUFFER FAILURE.
HURRY, VADER! PLEASE!

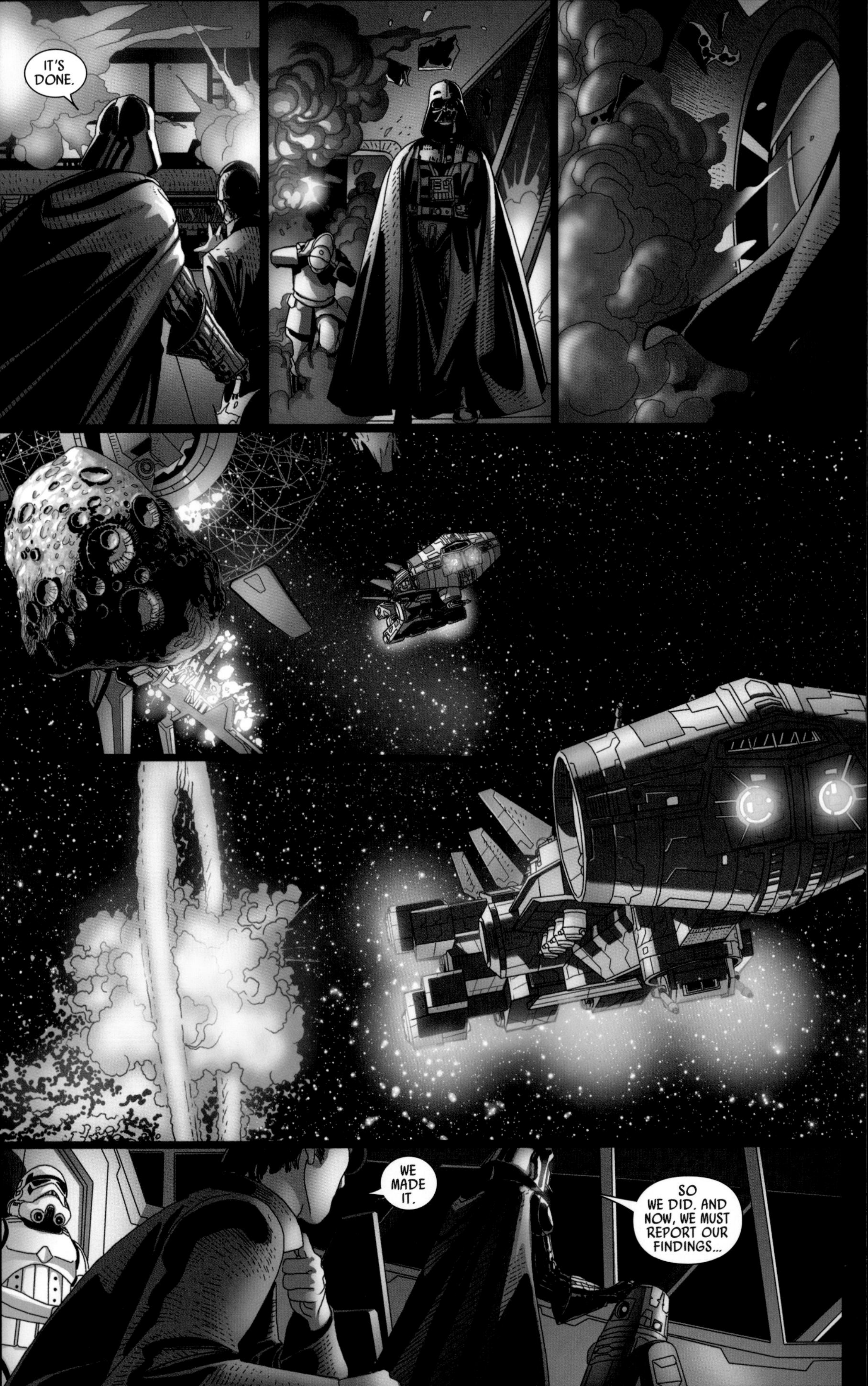
IT'S DONE.
WE MADE IT.
SO WE DID. AND NOW, WE MUST REPORT OUR FINDINGS...

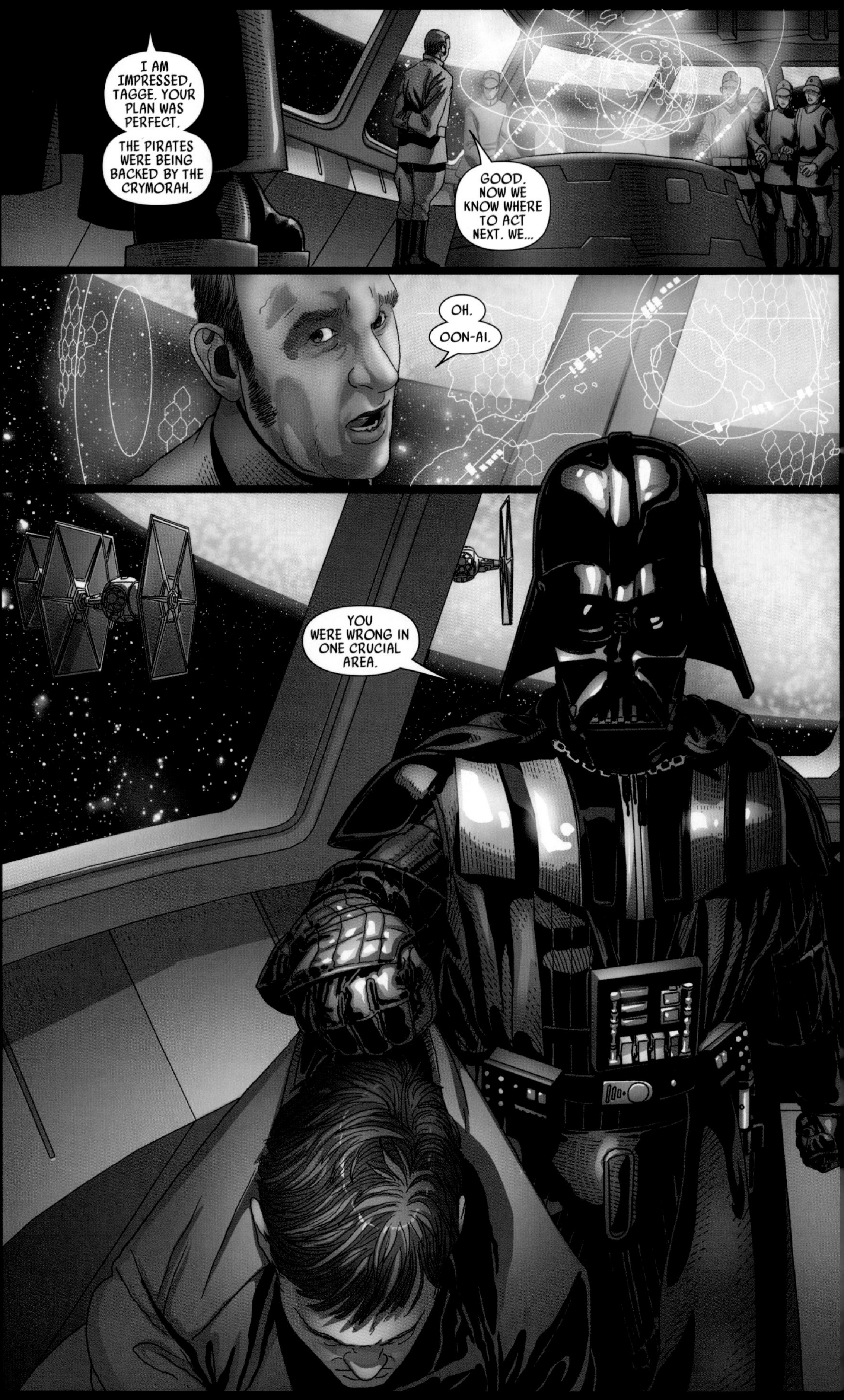
I AM IMPRESSED, TAGGE. YOUR PLAN WAS PERFECT.
THE PIRATES WERE BEING BACKED BY THE CRYMORAH.
GOOD. NOW WE KNOW WHERE TO ACT NEXT. WE...
OH.
OON-AI.
YOU WERE WRONG IN ONE CRUCIAL AREA.

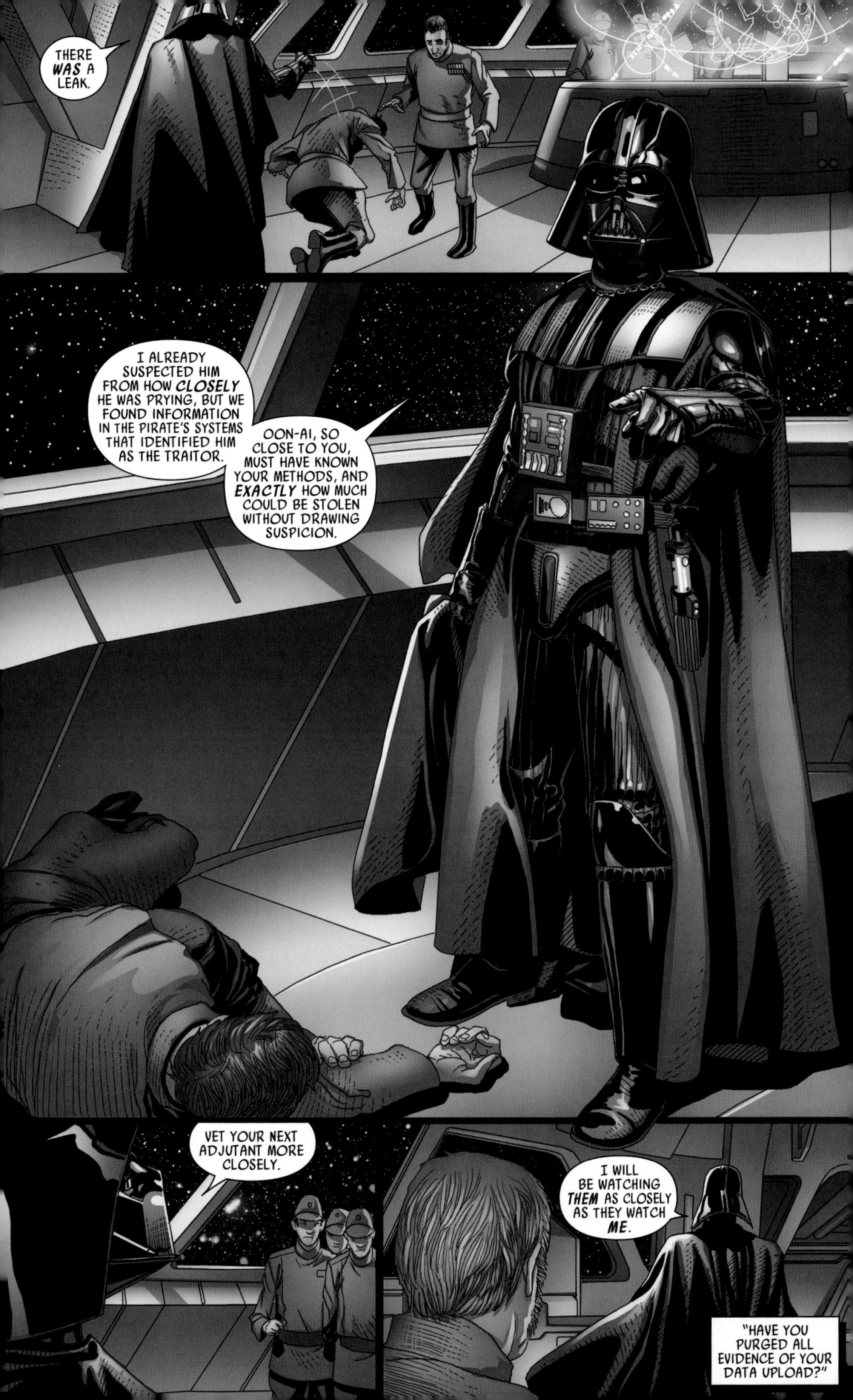
THERE WAS A LEAK.
I ALREADY SUSPECTED HIM FROM HOW CLOSELY HE WAS PRYING, BUT WE FOUND INFORMATION IN THE PIRATE'S SYSTEMS THAT IDENTIFIED HIM AS THE TRAITOR.
OON-AI, SO CLOSE TO YOU, MUST HAVE KNOWN YOUR METHODS, AND EXACTLY HOW MUCH COULD BE STOLEN WITHOUT DRAWING SUSPICION.
VET YOUR NEXT ADJUTANT MORE CLOSELY.
I WILL BE WATCHING THEM AS CLOSELY AS THEY WATCH ME.
"HAVE YOU PURGED ALL EVIDENCE OF YOUR DATA UPLOAD?"

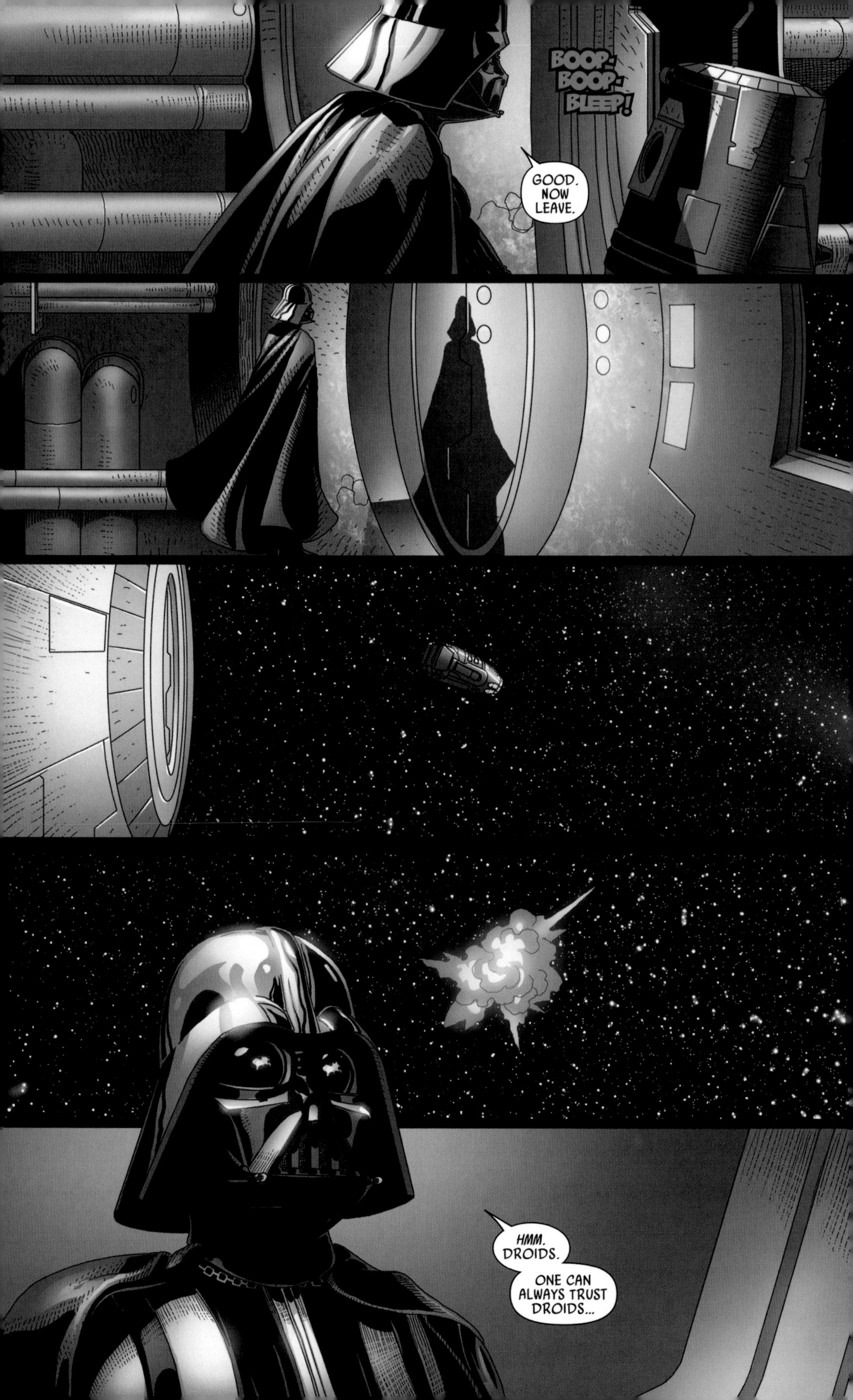
BOOP-BOOP-BLEEP!
GOOD. NOW LEAVE.
HMM. DROIDS.
ONE CAN ALWAYS TRUST DROIDS...

STAR WARS®

DARTH VADER

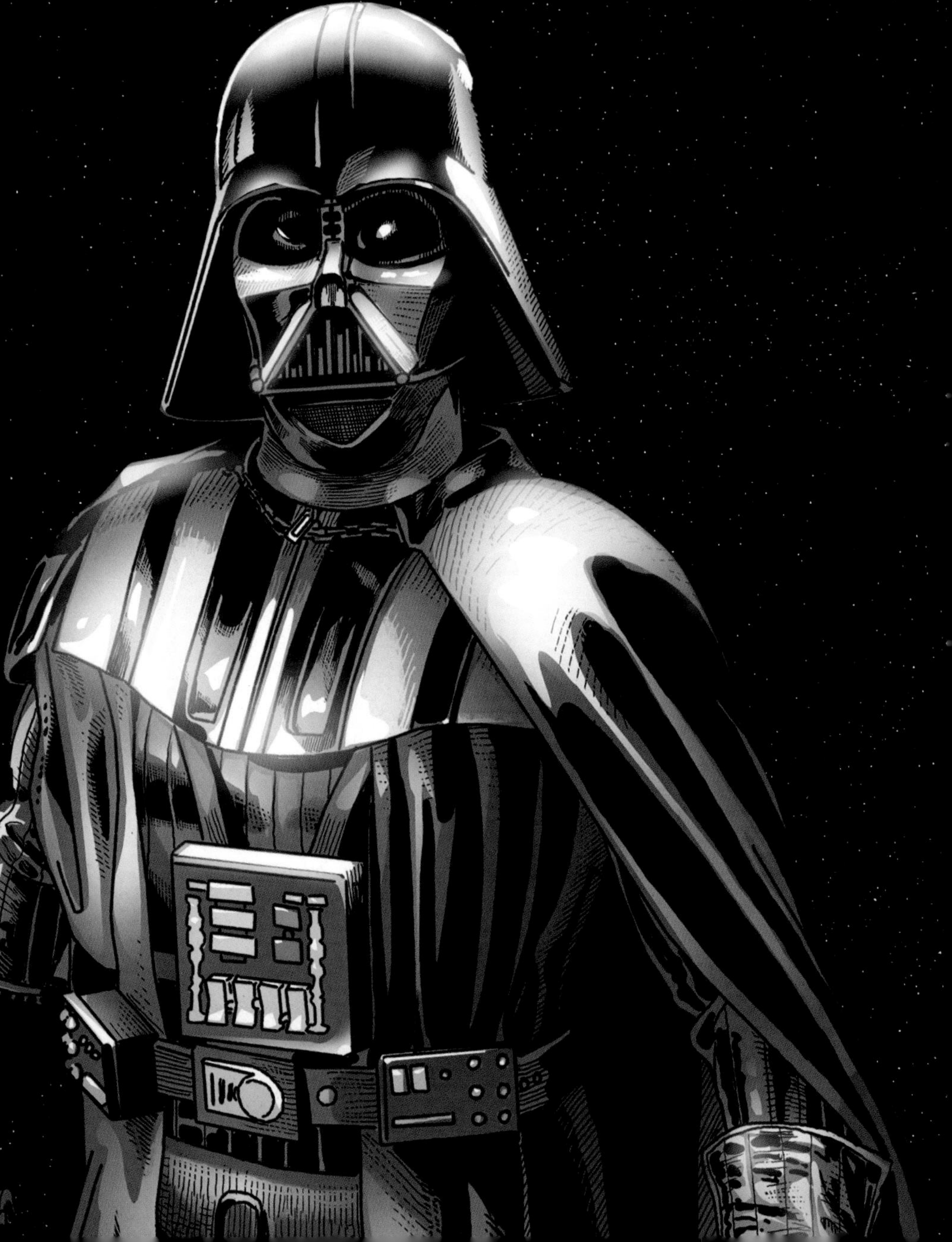

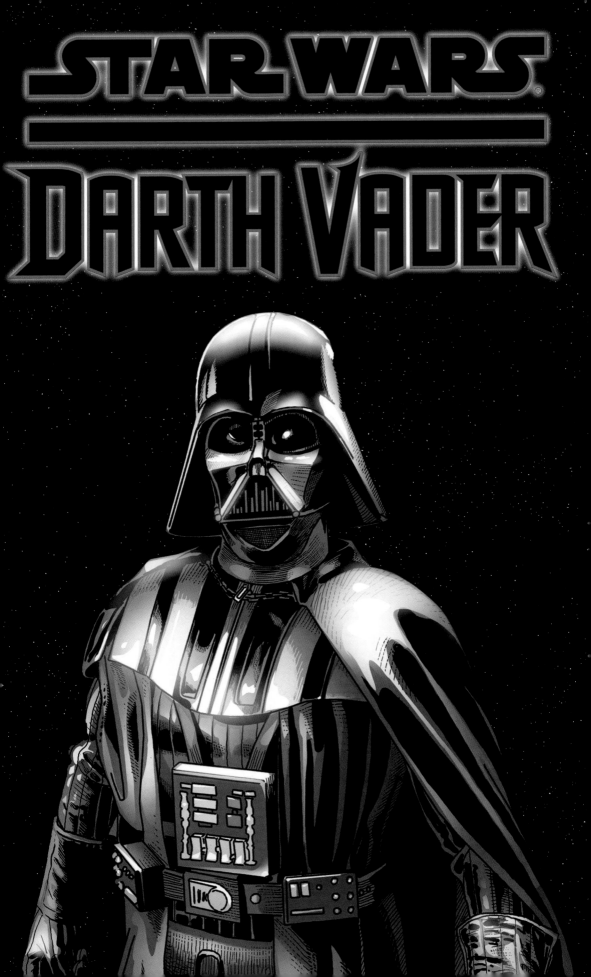

STAR WARS DARTH VADER

COLLECT THEM ALL!

Set of 6 Hardcover Books ISBN: 978-1-61479-519-3

STAR WARS
STAR WARS
DARTH VADER
VADER: VOLUME 1
GILLEN LARROCA DELGADO

Hardcover Book ISBN
978-1-61479-520-9

STAR WARS
STAR WARS
DARTH VADER
VADER: VOLUME 2
GILLEN LARROCA DELGADO

Hardcover Book ISBN
978-1-61479-521-6

STAR WARS
STAR WARS
DARTH VADER
VADER: VOLUME 3
GILLEN LARROCA DELGADO

Hardcover Book ISBN
978-1-61479-522-3

STAR WARS
STAR WARS
DARTH VADER
VADER: VOLUME 4
GILLEN LARROCA DELGADO

Hardcover Book ISBN
978-1-61479-523-0

STAR WARS
STAR WARS
DARTH VADER
VADER: VOLUME 5
GILLEN LARROCA DELGADO

Hardcover Book ISBN
978-1-61479-524-7

STAR WARS
STAR WARS
DARTH VADER
VADER: VOLUME 6
GILLEN LARROCA DELGADO

Hardcover Book ISBN
978-1-61479-525-4

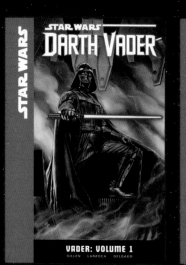

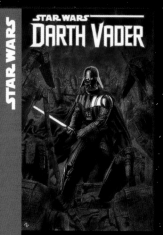

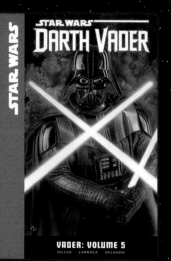